Frederick Wilson Kittermaster

Rhuddlan Castle

And other Poems

Frederick Wilson Kittermaster

Rhuddlan Castle
And other Poems

ISBN/EAN: 9783744770323

Printed in Europe, USA, Canada, Australia, Japan

Cover: Foto ©Andreas Hilbeck / pixelio.de

More available books at **www.hansebooks.com**

RHUDDLAN CASTLE,

AND OTHER POEMS.

BY THE

REV. FRED. W. KITTERMASTER, M.A.

(RHOWYNEDD.)

Coventry:

CURTIS & BEAMISH, PRINTERS AND PUBLISHERS.

—

1890.

CONTENTS.

Rhuddlan Castle.

A Poem which obtained the First Prize for English Verse at Rhuddlan Royal Eisteddfod, 1850.

" His wandering step,
Obedient to high thoughts, had visited
The awful ruins of the days of old."
Shelley.

" 'Tis but a remnant of the wreck of years."
Byron.

HUSH'D is the lyre that woke of yore
　　The swell of song from shore to shore;
Cold is the hand that touched the string
And still the voice once wont to sing.
By Conway's stream—from Snowdon's brow
No hallow'd strain is floating now,
The muse is lost, or gone;
Where erst the deepest theme was poured,
Where erst the God inspired adored,
Now silence reigns alone.
The tyrant's law has swept away
With cruel hand and ruthless sway
The Bard and bardic skill.

A

Well knew the tyrant that the breast
Where freedom reigned would never rest
While strangers o'er his native land
With haughty threat and proud command
Ruled with a lawless will.
He knew the Bard's loved theme too well,
Its mighty power, its mystic swell.
He feared the hand and voice whose strain
Could wake brave deeds to life again,
And bear the soul along ;
So cruel went the stern decree
To quench the flame that would be free,
And hush the bardic song.
Alas, that it has passed away !
I would the lyre were mine,
Of [1] "Taliesin," or the lay
Less gifted, yet Divine,
Since I would noble deeds rehearse,
And weave a song in simple verse.
For as from Rhuddlan's Castle steep
I watched the setting sun
Gild gloriously the distant deep,
His journey almost done ;
And on the mountains far and wide,
From Snowdon's range to Dyserth's side,
Saw golden lightnings run ;

And Clwyd's Vale grow dim as night
Spread silently her gems so bright;
A vision of old time came by
On pinions free and fast,
And for a moment let the eye
Gaze on the vanished past;
The past which from the memory fades,
And hides itself in darkest shades.

Wild breaks the scene! huge mountains rise
Whose snow-clad summits kiss the skies.
Dread winter's gloom and clouds are spread
On lofty peak and chasm dread.
Mad swollen torrents downward leap,
And raging floods the valleys sweep;
While Ædan holds his wrested power
Securely in his guarded tower.
But spring comes on with light and song,
Which revels those wild hills among,
With fresh'ning breath and opening bloom,
That laughs away cold winter's gloom,
And hastening on through dell and range
Throws over Nature's face a change.

Wake, ²Ædan, for thy short repose
Is broken by advancing foes!

With Nature's change a change will come
In thy securely-guarded home.
Whence is that swelling sound from far—
The clash of arms—the shout of war?
From southern climes, from southern shores,
A mighty host its numbers pours
The northern hills among.
A Prince renowned for warlike deeds,
From Rhoderic sprung, [3]Llewelyn leads
This troop as tempest strong.
Wake, Ædan! ere it be too late;
Check if thou canst thy adverse fate,
Make all thy strongholds stronger still,
Seize every pass, crown every hill,
Draw out thy troops in skilled array,
The strife is for thy crown to-day.

'Tis past! the shout, the battle's sound,
The rush—the cry of pain.
Pale Ædan and his sons are found
Among the mangled slain.
Llewelyn's banner waves on high,
All proudly 'gainst a cloudless sky,
Till sets the sun, as suns will set,
And glories pass away:
Till night makes silent the regret

And triumph of the day ;
And comes in mournful garb to spread
Her mantle o'er the ghastly dead.

Now peace returns, and with it brings
Llewelyn to the throne of kings,
Reared and made firm in days of old
By princes wise and warriors bold :
Whereon through ages reigned in state
The good, the noble, brave and great.
In quick succession comes each name
Emblazoned on the roll of fame ;
Renowed for deeds by minstrels sung,
From Royal Trojan ᵗBrutus sprung.
And now the brave Llewelyn wields
This sceptre won on battle fields.
And wields it wisely—plenty there
And prosperous times the people share.

Such the far age when Rhuddlan saw
Her noble castle rise !
To keep the plains around in awe,
And towering towards the skies,
Frown on the hostile bands from far
To check them in the path of war.
No want of zeal—no dull delay

Holds back the work begun,
United they wear out the day,
Nor rest till all is done ;
Advancing the huge towers are seen,
The massive walls creep up between,
And zeal untired the fabric rears
Till threatening o'er the plains
The finished Castle's form appears
Where Prince Llewelyn reigns.

'Tis all complete, and peace succeeds,
And blessings spread around ;
No army for its country bleeds,
No slaughter stains the ground.
Full plenty with a bounteous hand
Spreads joy and hope throughout the land,
And summers come and summers fly,
And no dark cloud pollutes the sky,
Till ⁵Meyrick spreads a gloom ;
Brief as the shade of April day
It comes, but quickly flies away,
For Meyrick meets his doom.
With flashing blade and deadly blow
The brave Llewelyn lays him low.
The traitor's hopes—the traitor's breath,
Are buried in the sleep of death.

Fair Rhuddlan Castle's halls are bright,
For revelry is there ;
Llewelyn gives a feast to-night
To noble, brave and fair.
A banquet sumptuously is spread
With choicest fruits—the wine is red,
The guests are there ; each beaming eye
Grows brighter with the revelry ;
Gladness and joyous laughter sound,
The pledging cup goes quickly round,
As they the night prolong.
But why that hush ? that sudden fall
Of mirth ? what echoes through the hall ?
Hark ! 'tis the swell of song !
The Bard has struck the sacred lyre,
The Bard awaits poetic fire
To breathe in numbers strong.
What does he sing in lofty strain ?
Of ⁶Rhun defeated, or the slain,
The noble and the brave that lie
With stiffened form and dim set eye,
Upon the battlefield ;
Of rare exploits and deeds that gave
New honours to the conquering brave
Who know not how to yield ?
He sings of brave Llewelyn's deeds ;

He sings of love and fame ;
The all-attentive ear he feeds,
And fans the lighted flame.
Absorbed, each arm renews its might,
Each foot stands firm in bloody fight,
No maiden pleads in vain ;
Ere long she must in safety be,
The wrong avenged, the captive free,
Or they among the slain.
They dream of battle, love, renown,
Of fame's deep voice, of glory's crown ;
Nor think they of the coming day—
The Bard has borne the soul away.

Llewelyn's reign has passed away :
The traitor laid him low ;
Ambition showed the bloody way,
While envy struck the blow.
Why, Rhuddlan, does another now
Rule thy proud towers ?—thy vassals bow
Not to thy founder's son,
Nor to the traitor, who would gain
By bloody deeds a throne, and reign
O'er lands so foully won.
Where sleeps the spirit of the sire ?
Where slumbers brave Llewelyn's fire,

That mighty deeds has done ?
It wakes, for ⁷Grufydd feels the flame.
In warrior's garb he comes to claim
His noble father's throne.
King Edwal's son fears not the strife,
But seeks the battle plain—
He yields the sceptre with his life
And lies among the slain.

How shall I sing thy festive halls
In Gryffyth's reign all bright ;
What time oft rung the echoing walls
With praises of his might ?
When Dane and Saxon routed fled,
And Severn's banks were strewn with dead ?
When ⁸Howel bid the fight farewell,
And Edwyn bravely fighting fell ?
When from each field the conqueror came
With added spoils—with added fame ?
Then were thy halls all bright and gay,
Then gladly passed the joyous day
With happiness and song.
Passed quickly by ! Too soon, alas !
Our joyous days and pleasures pass—
We seldom hold them long.
So have I seen the sunset fade

From living light to purple shade.
So have I seen that blaze of light
Along the western sky
So full, so glorious in its might,
It seemed too bright to die —
Grow dim as spread the dusky night
Her sable plumes on high.

There spreads a rumour that the foe
With hostile purpose come
To lay proud Rhuddlan's Castle low,
And seize the King at home.
Fly ⁹Grufydd ! for thy safety fly !
Brave Harold and his troops are nigh ;
Thou canst not stem his gath'ring might :
Thy safety lies alone in flight.
'Tis wisely done !   The favouring breeze ·
Shall bear thee from thy foes ;
Look not behind across the seas
Upon thy country's woes.
Fair Rhuddlan's towers are wreathed in flame !
The conqueror in his fury came
To seize with vengeful hand
His rival chief ; but finds thy halls
Kingless and lone ; so vengeance falls
On thy devoted land.

Take the glad wreath from off thy brow,
Thy castle is dismantled now.

Mourn Rhuddlan, o'er thy humbled pride,
Thy Castle overthrown !
The fire has scorched its bulky side,
And rent the massive stone.
Its lofty turrets strew the ground,
Its haughty towers are scattered round ;
Low in the dust its strength is laid,
Its glories in the distance fade,
The conqueror boasts his power ;
No friendly hand can help afford ;
No rumour of thy absent Lord
To succour in this hour.
Oh ! for Llewelyn's sword to-day
To aid thy cause—the wreck to stay !
Thy honour to redeem, and smite
The smiter with the sword of might !
But this no more is thine !
To royal [10]Edwyn's valiant son,
Renowned in fight for glories won,
Thou must thyself resign.

Time flies ! again thy turrets rise,
Thy threatening form the foe defies,

Thy finished towers are seen from far
A safe retreat in pressing war,
Too safe to let them rest.
The Norman [10]William fears thy might,
A fortress strong in bloody fight,
A home for the distrest.
The mandate comes ; thou must resign
All that by gentle right is thine ;
For gentle right and justice fail
Where Norman laws and might prevail ;
The conqueror needs thy aid
To strengthen his yet doubtful cause,
To stablish those unwelcome laws
By stern invaders made ;
And Norman zeal and Norman skill
Make strong thy towers 'gainst coming ill.

Who breaks the gentle peace that reigns ?
Who troubles now the State ?
Who shakes with troops the yielding plains
And thunders at thy gates?
'Tis David valiant Gwynedd's son
Who with a chosen band
Comes to avenge foul deeds oft done,
And free his father-land :
To bid the savage conqueror fly,

Or yield before his might and die.
'Tis vain ! [11]King Henry fears the blow,
And brings his succours to the foe ;
Checks David's zeal and purpose dire,
And makes him to the hills retire.
Drives far thy fear and brings relief,
And with it gladness ; but how brief,
How soon shall cease thy song !
From Berwyn's heights the king has fled,
Unchecked around thy castle spread
New forces ten-fold strong.
There [12]Owen Gwynedd's banner flies,
The North to represent ;
There Southern Rhys his aid supplies,
On deeds heroic bent ;
And Madoc's sons, and Owen brave
That princely Powis sends
To seek for glory or a grave,
That to such glory tends :
These bid thee yield, who can withstand
The brave who for their own loved land
Will conquer, or will die ?
No Norman power,—no fortress strong
Can hold itself in safety long,
Nor such a host defy.

Fierce was the siege that cast thee down ;

But that has passed away.
Dismantled towers no longer frown
On wreck and slow decay.
Restored the free reign in thy halls,
The Bard awakes the strain ;
The fate of battle-fields recalls,
And mirth is thine again.
With rapid wing years hasten on,
Joy chases gloom, then both are gone.
And summers come and summers fly,
New hopes and fears spring up and die.
Now [13]Baldwin bids the nation rise
To fight the Christian's foe ;
Peace, home and all to sacrifice
Through foreign lands to go,
And raise the standard of the Cross,
And there redeem the Christian's loss.
Now [14]Chester's Earl defends thy walls
And keeps the foe at bay ;
Now fierce [15]Llewelyn on thee calls
To yield before his sway.
His power will make resistance vain,
The summons must be heard ;
Admit him to thy halls to reign,
Obey the conqueror's word.

Wake, Cambria ! heard ye not the sound !

The royal mandate flies
With swift untiring wing around
For troops and fresh supplies.
The haughty [16]Edward vengeance swears ;
A mighty host in wrath prepares
His cherished hopes to aid :
From far and near the succours come
To march into thy mountain home,
Thy country to invade.
Equipped for war ; in arms complete
On Rhuddlan's plains his forces meet ;
From Rhuddlan's towers restored and strong
His princely banner streams ;
In Rhuddlan's halls are light and song
Ambition and its dreams.

War, wasting war, unceasing reigns
On Cambria's hills, on Cambria's plains :
Dread fire and sword, revenge and hate
Make all the country desolate.
Llewelyn for a sceptre strives
Held free from time untold ;
From princely sires his claim derives
Through lineage true and old :
While Edward views with envious eye
The power that dare his arms defy ;

Fears the rude crags which let the foe
Breathe scorn upon his troops below ;
And seeks how he may best enslave
A people unsubdued and brave.

Mourn Cambria ! mourn thy fallen state !
[17]Llewelyn is no more !
In dismal strain bewail his fate
From shore to distant shore.
With him thy ruined fortunes lie,
With him hope's promises must die !
Strong was his father's lofty hold
Upon the mountain high,
Where with his followers free and bold
He could a host defy ;
There he might hold his foe at bay
And keep his throne secure for aye.
Why did he then with spirit brave
Descend his country's rights to save ?
It was a luckless hour,
When trusting traitorous hearts in vain,
He dared come down upon the plain,
From lofty Penmaen Mawr.
Mourn Cambria o'er thy fortunes fled,
Thy last, thy bravest Prince is dead !

In Rhuddlan Edward proudly reigns,

And strips the conquered land ;
His troops victorious scour the plains ;
None dare his arms withstand ;
The proudest now are forced to cower,
And every stronghold own his power.
Last, steep [18]Dol'ddelan yields :
O'er hill and dale, o'er dell and wood ;
O'er Lledr's stream, and Conway's flood
The sceptre now he wields.
And Rhuddlan's halls are festive now,
The wreath is on the conqueror's brow :
A thousand ready tongues are found
His fame to tell—his praise to sound ;
But who will boldly crave
In that glad hour of conquest proud
When swell congratulations loud
A pardon for the brave ?
No voice for gentle mercy plead !
No voice with justice intercedes,
The fallen great to save !
So deeds th' invaded dare devise
That blot ambition's reign.
Lo ! [19]David in the dungeon sighs,
And makes requests in vain ;
Hark ! the dread shriek of murder flies
Across the troubled plain ;

B

From [20]Menai's shores upon the blast
The Bard's last wail is hurried past.
Pause Edward ! for upon thy name
Which conquests now adorn,
Such deeds will write undying shame,
In ages yet unborn.

But this is o'er !—thy mean [21]deceit
The pomp and regal state ;
The Bardic wail with woe replete,
And David's wretched fate :
All this is past, and let it die
With thee, and in oblivion lie.
But Rhuddlan's towers have seen a change,
And heard the voice of woe ;
In [22]Richard's fall how fortunes change,
And crowns may come and go.
Have seen a change, and felt the power
That raged in mad rebellion's hour ;
Beheld the tide they could not quell
And yielding to its fury fell.

So passes earthly greatness by,
So earthly glories fade and die.
How grand were Rhuddlan's walls of yore,
But grandeur smiles on them no more.

How glorious in her former day,
How gloomy now her ruins grey.
Decay and death bring wreck and shade,
Earth's proudest monuments must fade.
Years glide along on time's swift stream,
Life's brightest joys are but a dream.
To some how short! a tinted ray
That in a vapour melts away.
How fleeting, false, unreal, dead,
Will earth appear when life has sped.
The glare that now attracts the eye,
The rank for which men toil and die,
The passions which corrupt the taste,
And health and strength and beauty waste.
The revel mad, the godless mirth,
The pomp and pageantry of earth.
When life is past, what will they seem?
But phantom shapes, a fitful dream :
A fitful dream, that will not stay ;
But vanish in eternal day.

Naaman the Syrian.

BESIDE the Prophet's dwelling,
   Nigh Carmel's sacred hill,
A company are resting,
   Their chariot wheels are still :
A grand imposing pageant
   In expectation waits,
For Syria's mighty Captain
   Is at the Prophet's gates.

He bears his costly presents,
   And royal words he brings ;
Assured of hearty welcome,
   The favoured guest of kings.
He, Naaman the Syrian,
   For prowess known afar ;
He, Naaman the Syrian,
   The victor chief in war !

Why stands he thus a suppliant?
   What does he come to crave?
Whose voice could bid destruction,
   Whose spoken word could save.
Proud Naaman the Syrian,
   With iron strength and will,
Is Naaman the Leper,
   And needs the Prophet's skill.

Unheeding all his greatness,
   His royal mandate shown,—
The Prophet owns no Master,
   Obeys no earthly throne.
The power of inspiration,
   Breathed by the Prophet's Lord,
And Naaman the Syrian
   Hears this commanding word.

Go! wash in flowing Jordan!
   Go! wash, and it shall be,
When seven times repeated,
   Thy flesh shall come to thee!
And in his quiet chamber
   The man of God remains;
Not seeking royal favour,
   Nor asking earthly gains.

" Methought," the angry Syrian
  Replied, " that he would stand,
And calling on his Master,
  Strike with a Prophet's hand.
Strike o'er the place infected,
  And bid the poison cease ;
Then might the cleansèd Leper
  Return again in peace.

"Lo ! Abana and Pharpar
  Are rivers better still
Than all the rippling streamlets
  That make up Jordan's rill.
Why not in their broad waters,
  Bright with the morning's sheen,
Dip seven times the Leper,
  And make the Leper clean ? "

"My Father, if the Prophet,"
  So gentler voices sway,
" Had bid thee do some great thing,
  Wouldest thou not obey ?
Why not, then, in this smaller,
  That needs not strength nor skill,
In all that he commandeth
  Obey the Prophet's will ? "

Beside the flowing Jordan,
　Upon its golden sands,
In changed and lowly posture
　The humbled Leper stands :
And seven times he dips him,
　And finds the lucid wave
Has at the Prophet's bidding
　The cleansing power to save.

Not by the mighty actions
　Which spring from human thought;
Not by earth's great exertions
　Are heavenly blessings bought ;
But in God's own appointment,
　A sure and simple way,
Are life and health and safety
　To all who will obey.

There in the means provided
　The grace of God is found ;
There every earnest effort
　Is by His goodness crowned ;
There penitent and pleading,
　A broken heart within,
The soul shall feel no longer
　The leprosy of sin.

1865.

Birthday Lines for Rose.

Written when crossing the Atlantic Ocean on my way to America, May 9th, 1866.

I FEEL the heaving sea below,
  I hear old Ocean's song;
The waves are dancing to and fro,
  Our vessel speeds along.

The crest foam sparkles in the sun,
  The rainbows deck the spray;
The fleecy clouds their courses run,
  And brightly shines the day.

But far across the briny tide
  The fancy dreaming goes
Down by the winding 'Tanat's side,
  The quiet home of Rose.

I greet thee in thy quiet home,
  Thou "Queen of flowers!" and send
Backward with yon receding tide
  A thought with thine to blend.

Thy girlish years have passed away
  On time's unceasing flood,
And brighter, fairer, day by day,
  Dawns comelier womanhood.

What shall I wish ? That every grace
  Within thy heart may reign ;
That spared for years in life's swift race,
  This day to greet again ;

Thy home may ever happier be,
  Thy days all brighter shine,
Thy love be hers who doats on thee,
  Whose life is wrapp'd in thine.

May He Who rules the land and sea
  Thy course in life defend ;
And many, many blessings be
  Thy portion to its end.

Spring Memories.

WAS it a dream—that breath of Spring
    Which came and went in days gone by,
And now the waking mem'ry brings,
    When light was in the sky?

Was it a dream—that murm'ring sound
    Of Tanat rising up the hill,
Mingling with Nature's voice around,
    When all beside was still?

Too marked—too real for a dream!
    I feel the breath, the light I see;
I hear the sound of Tanat's stream,
    And all comes back to me.

I look across the valley—green
    With springing grass; while opening flowers
Smile in the scented morning sheen,
    Along the hedge-row bowers.

The winding river rolls along,
    The greedy trout leaps at the fly;
I listen to the ceaseless song,
    And yet I heave a sigh.

A creeping shadow seems to come
  Across the way I roamed anon ;
From yonder peaceful nestling home
  The brighter light has gone.

Perchance a passing shade that lies
  Too darkly on the silver past,
Again to vanish from life's skies,
  And leave them clear at last.

'Tis not all wise to think *that* best,
  Though fair and joyous, if it die ;
There is a truer, sweeter rest
  Beside God's throne on high.

'Tis not all wise to dream on time
  As if it never passed away ;
Beyond it is the life sublime
  In God's eternal day.

If led to this by changes here,
  And passing clouds, then we shall stand,
As comes again the opening year,
  Nearer the promised land.

Till faintly through the closing night
  Of death, we see our home above,
And know that we shall rise to light,
  And joy, and peace, and love.

To Mr. & Mrs. Darlington,

OF BOURTON HALL,

On their Silver Wedding, Sept. 4th, 1886.

SOFT light breaks with the morning
    As silver lightnings fly,
From night's dim murky chambers,
    Across the changing sky :
Pale azure still grows deeper,
    As shadows pass away.
And sits the sun in splendour
    Upon the throne of day.

From Winter's dreary slumber
    Fresh balmy Spring awakes,
And from earth's frozen shoulders
    Its icy mantle shakes :
With silent hand she touches
    Each bud, and flower, and weaves
A living dress for summer
    With her ten thousand leaves.

To Mr. and Mrs. Darlington.

As morn gives place to noonday,
　So noonday to the night.
The mid-day sun goes downward,
　To set in living light ;
More beautiful in dying
　Among his crimson fires ;
Breathed in intenser glory
　Ere the great king expires.

As Spring gives place to Summer,
　So Summer must again
Give place to fruitful Autumn,
　All rich in golden grain.
Then slow decay creeps onward
　Beneath calm cloudless skies ;
Till shrouded in cold winter
　All vegetation dies.

Thus all is moving forward
　On time's resistless tide.
From infancy comes manhood ;
　From a babe the blushing bride.
And joined in holy union
　As one, for weal or woe,
Along the doubtful journey
　Of chequered life they go.

'Tis now the noon-tide Summer
   With you as man and wife.
Domestic joys are all around,
   And crown your married life.
It is your silver wedding,
   And through the vanished years
The guidance and the blessing
   Of God's Providence appears.

No need to fight life's battle,
   Nor labour's war to wage ;
Your lot has fallen pleasantly,
   A goodly heritage.
Your quiver full—like arrows
   In a mighty giant's hand,
Your glory and your safety,
   Your children round you stand.

Lo ! Hayward, of such promise,
   With tastes refined and good ;
And Lady-bird, so charming,
   On the verge of womanhood ;
And Maude, with lustrous beauty
   In all its winning grace ;
And Mopsy, calm and thoughtful,
   But with deeply speaking face ;

Then tall Lucy and fair Agnes,
  Not to pass them by ;
And quick, light-hearted Connie,
  With dark and flashing eye ;
And Willoughby, though last, not least,
  In life to play his part,
Who holds a secret corner
  In his mother's loving heart.

One thought alone of sadness
  Comes to you from the hill,
Where lies your absent darling,
  'Neath the marble cold and still.
'Twas well ! for He Who never errs,
  But rules all for the best,
Cut down the flower He wanted
  For its everlasting rest.

'Twas well ! you know not now, but yet
  You shall hereafter know
Why this little one was taken,
  Though so hard to let him go.
To draw you, perhaps, to better things,
  And lift your thoughts above
To where he now is happy,
  In the home of light and love.

We greet you with good wishes,
　And may this wedding be
All silvery with bright faces
　And glad festivity ;
Without one anxious thought or care,
　Without one boding sigh,
May all be clear and beautiful
　On life's unclouded sky.

Look forward to the future !
　We wish you many years
Of tranquil joy and happiness,
　Unmixed with earthly fears.
That when the five-and-twenty
　Shall again have passed away,
You may keep your *golden wedding*
　As you keep the one to-day.

And see your children's children,
　A bonnie, happy train ;
And hear their gladsome voices
　To make you young again ;
And waken olden memories,
　Before they pass away,
Of how you kept in former years
　Your silver wedding day.

Look forward to the future !
  For years are rolling on,
And all that is around us now
  Will change, or soon be gone ;
Life's noonday and life's summer
  Will hasten down the steep,
And lie almost forgotten
  In death's unbroken sleep.

Look forward to the future !
  Beyond the gloomy line
Where death appears in terrors
  Immortal glories shine ;
There is the home most blessed,
  There be your rest at last ;
When all life's joys and sorrows
  Shall lie buried in the past.

----

c

"Killarney Boat Song.

I HEARD the water's music
    When speeding o'er the lake;
I heard its spirit speaking
    As the wild waves round us brake,
And with free and restless motion
    Went sparkling far away
To the freshness of the breezes,
    And the light of Summer's day.

But they spoke to me of something
    When the day's work should be done,
And the crimson tide of glory
    Should surround the setting sun;
When the sparkle and the freshness
    And the motion should subside—
Of the calm unruffled beauty
    Of the golden eventide.

I heard some voices blending
  Which a deeper meaning gave
To the chanting of the waters
  And the breaking of the wave :
They were the young heart's music,
  Fresh from its gushing springs,
When the future seems all joyous,
  And hope its visions brings.

Yet they spoke to me of something
  When this life should be o'er,
And those voices in their sweetness
  Should blend on earth no more ;
When the young heart's deepest feelings
  And gushing springs should cease—
Of the rest that is in Jesus,
  And deep eternal peace.

Earth is changing—it is changing,
  All its pleasures pass away !
It is changing—it is changing,
  Like the beauty of the day !
From its fashion that decayeth
  Let us lift our thoughts on high,
To where beauty is unfading,
  And pleasures never die.

To Rose.

THE thoughts go flitting to and fro,
  As comes the scented Spring-time breeze,
And genial sunbeams dancing go
  Among the budding trees.

They catch the life which Nature brings,
  When waking from her Winter rest,
On balmy air she spreads her wings
  In softest plumage drest.

And heedless, too, of time or space,
  Along the pathway of the past
They run a joyous, free wild race,
  Where'er life's lot was cast.

That pathway set with hopes and fears,
  Fulfill'd, or rudely put to flight;
And fading as the mist of years
  Creeps on with darker night.

But there are golden threads which run
  Through all the past, if view'd aright ;
Like streamlets in the Summer sun,
  Which make the landscape bright.

The golden threads of that great love
  Of Him Who kept us day by day ;
And watched us from His throne above,
  Lest we should go astray.

Not chance, but His sure guiding hand,
  Has brought us to the present hour ;
And now in life we only stand
  By His protecting power.

All things were made, both dark and light,
  To work our good, and so we still
Shall find upon the darkness light
  By His all ruling will.

We see but dimly now ! The way
  He leads may not appear the best ;
Yet we shall find some future day
  It led to endless rest.

And as the clouds go flitting by
   Across the shining noon-tide glare,
But leave no mark upon the sky
   'To tell that they were there.

So shall the stormy clouds which lie
   Upon life's sky be put to flight ;
Nor leave a stain, but fade and die
   In God's resplendent light.

And then the truest rest will come,
   When all released from earthly strife,
We wake at length in that bright home
   Of blissful endless life.

———————

October Verses

At the [25] *Royal Oak, Bettws-y-Coed,* 1866.

I USED to come to Bettws
  Some fifteen years ago ;
The "Oak" was then a pleasant place
  With Creswick, Cox, and Co. ;
But then no restless tourists
  Were rushing to and fro.

The ground was all artistic ;
  Down by that quaint old mill
Would sit some candidate for fame,
  Another on the hill
Among the heathered moorland ;
  I would it were so still.

Some wand'ring fisherman, perchance,
  The solitude would break,
By rock-bound foaming Llugwy,
  Or swift Lledr ; or would take
" Big trouts " in stormy weather
  From Moel Siabod's lake.

Or some stout tired pedestrian
  At eventide would stay
To rest his weary limbs awhile ;
  And then at break of day,
To climb the lofty mountain
  With new vigour start away.

And then sat landlord Roberts
  Upon the settle there ;
And that most portly gentleman,
  Old Hoyle, upon a chair ;
Both drinking strongest waters
  To drive away dull care.

Methinks I see the Doctor,
  John Fogg, and little Bach !
Hulme, Chattock, and brave Hallewell,
  And Cox on fame's steep track ;
And Tullock, whose wild dashes
  Artistic taste did lack !

And that snug little parlour
  Where we did meet of yore,
When numb'ring all our company
  We were not half-a-score ;
Where the brave maiden stood cartooned
  Life-size upon the door !

I come again to Bettws,
　　But all is changed, I trow :
The " Oak," that used to flourish once
　　Was quite a little bough,
Compared with the large branches
　　I see around me now.

There is no longer quiet—
　　The Tourists now are here ;
They are a noisy company
　　And like a goodly cheer ;
They laugh, and shout, and chatter,
　　Drink stout and bitter beer.

The Swallow Falls they visit ;
　　To Conway's flood they go ;
Look over Pont-y-Pair awhile,
　　Crack jokes with So-and-so ;
And having done old Bettws,
　　Post back to Llandudno.

But still true art doth flourish,
　　And genius must endure
This constant rush of visitors,
　　A thing it cannot cure ;
We see the earnest Student
　　And meet the Amateur.

There's Leche, down in Fosse Nodden,
  Now called the Fairy Glen,
Intent on his great master-piece,
  A work for fame ; but then
He'd rather be a grousing
  Upon the hills I ken.

And Reed, with his rheumatics ;
  They will not let him be ;
They touch him 'tween his shoulders,
  And twitch him in the knee,
And sorely spoil his relish
  For pleasant company.

And Leader seeks Glyn Lledr,
  So wonderful in form ;
All glorious in the setting sun
  When Summer nights are warm ;
But grand in its rough beauty
  Beneath the frowning storm.

There Jackson also wanders
  Those fairy scenes among ;
So skilled to touch the light guitar,
  And wake the swell of song ;
His soul all full of music
  While sauntering along.

But Eastlake just has left us ;
    I think it was not wise,
When came the bright fine weather,
    And Autumn's cloudless skies :
And with him charming Fluffy,
    And Dolly's laughing eyes.

And Agg comes from the river,
    All through the rain and mist ;
There's something in that salmon sport
    These people can't resist.
And Whittaker drops in at night
    To play a game at whist.

Then Hawkins says tobacco
    Is a most noxious weed ;
And truth perchance is on his side,
    But greater powers he'll need
To check its rooted practice,
    And silence Leche and Reed.

And Bell, a right good fellow,
    Yet given to be late ;
Wells, Syer, Steeple, Emerson,
    All striving to be great ;
And Charlie in the bar-room
    With her eternal slate.

But in the "Oak" grown larger,
  We candidly must say,
There are more comforts at command
  Than in the former day :
For these we gladly will accord
  Our thanks to Mrs. Rae.

A Fragment.

FAIR was the morn at Oban's home,
  And clear the sleeping bay ;
Ocean had laid its angry foam
  And surging waves away :
While many a heart was glad and light,
  And beat with purpose true ;
And many an eye grew full and bright
  Beneath that sky of blue.

To Staffa's wondrous lonely isle,
  And old Iona's fane ;
By sunny rock and green defile,
  Along the western main,
The steamer ploughed her onward way
  Across the deep, deep sea ;
And from her bows the leaping spray
  Went rolling merrily.

he Ascent of Snowdon

From Bettws-y-Coed, 1866.

A WAKE ! the rosy fragrant morn
  Has chased away the murky dawn.
Shake from your eyelids drowsy sleep,
We climb to-day old Snowdon's steep,
To view the landscape far and wide
From Berwyn's heights to ocean's tide !
Come ! breakfast waits, and we must lay
A good substratum for the day !

" Eat what you can, but pocket none,"
So doth the olden proverb run.
But here we seem to eat and cram
Into our satchels beef and ham
For mountain lunch, when air and height
Have whet our earthly appetite.
But one, more dainty than the rest,
Has slices from a chicken's breast ;
The better for her health and weal—
'Tis charming Fluffy's mid-day meal.

Oh—what a name! I wonder where
They found it for a girl so fair,
With soft, rich, sunny, golden hair !

We start—and Bettws leave behind,
And Capel Curig too ;
Where Robin can two ponies find,
And promises a view :
Smooth-spoken guide, I am inclined
To think your words untrue !

From Pen-y-Pass, both sure and slow,
Along the mountain path we go,
And Helen leads the way ;
All stately on her sable steed,
No guide nor aid she seems to need,
And fresh and bright to-day.
With beaming countenance and fair,
Ah ! of her maiden smile beware,
For 'tis a dangerous thing ;
When hearts are light and spirits high
With no dark cloud on life's clear sky,
And love is on the wing,
To feel fond sympathy our own
Until we worship at its throne ;
To-morrow perhaps may leave us lone.

And Fluffy next, with spirits high,

Without one anxious care ;
So winning, with her lustrous eye
And streaming golden hair ;
No sadness makes her young heart sigh,
And sorrow sits not there.
Fair girl ! may life's rough pathway be
All clear, and smooth, and safe to thee !
May summer days unclouded bring
Serenest joys ! may hope's deep spring
Send up its waters pure and clear
To cheer thee onward year by year ;
And when life's days are past,
May'st thou lie gently down to rest
Securely on thy Saviour's breast,
And find true joy at last !
There only will earth's trouble cease,
There only can be perfect peace !

And last, not least, is Dolly seen,
A quiet, dark-eyed maiden queen,
So picturesque and staid ;
On stronger steed of heavier tread,
With jacket of a sombre red,
And skirt of darker shade.
I see from out her gleaming eye
The living, sunny glances fly—

I wonder where they rest!
Or where the thoughts in pensive hour,
Drawn by some sympathetic power,
Have made themselves a nest!
Methinks there is a home away
To which those thoughts and glances stray!

But rock, and steep, and danger past,
We reach the mountain top at last;
And expectation wakes anew
To catch the far extensive view.
How vain that hope! thick clouds are spread
Upon the rocky monarch's head.
So down we sit to eat, and munch
Our beef, and ham, and chicken lunch:
And then return, so ill repaid
For all the great exertion made.
But ere we go we take a look
And see how reads the stranger's book;
And leave our names among the rest;
And "verses" Fluffy doth suggest.

."We came to see! but see—alas!
Wherever is Llanberis Pass?
And Cwellin's Lake, and Aber's Bridge,
And distant Cader's lofty ridge;
And Moel Siabod's outline true

Against a summer sky of blue;
And slippery Glydr's broken forms,
Swept rudely by a thousand storms;
And boundless ocean wild and free,
And low, flat, sandy Anglesea!
And Menai's Straits with mighty span,
A trophy to the skill of man?
Alas! we cannot see to-day
More than a hundred yards away.
Each sunny gleam the clouds resist,
We've missed the view and viewed the mist.
We've braved alike the steep and bog
To gaze on a damp, sweeping fog.

They say the Muse can rise and soar,
And sing of things divine,
And make the listening soul adore;
This is no gift of mine!
At least not now, when hope is dead,
And morning's promises have fled.
I cannot even wake the strain
To tell how we got down again.
So I must cease—born out of time,
Not in the golden age,
I am no Muse, but only rhyme
Content as Fluffy's page.

D

Plas Hên Wedding.

TO CARRIE.

So when you left me lonely in the wood
I wandered onward to the summer seat ;
And as the waters playfully went by
I took some fitful thoughts from out my brain,
And wove them into rhyme. Such as they are
I lay them on thy shrine, and only ask
One smile approving now the work is done.

BRIGHT is the morning's dancing ray,
　　More dear than the broad blaze of day.
Sweet is the fragrant breath which soon
Dies in the burning sultry noon.
And glorious are those streams of light
Which sunset spreads on coming night.
They pass, as earthly things pass by,
Delight, then disappoint and die.
Bright, dazzling, beautiful, they last
A moment, vanish, and are past.
We vainly grasp their parting gleam,
And weave from real things a dream ;

This only stays—the vision yet
Still lingers, veiled in fond regret.
So with our joys ; they come and go,
And leave bright spots behind ;
Like islands in a sea of woe,
Rests for the troubled mind.
From airy heights we see them gleam
As sacred spots in time's broad stream ;
Far up the vale of years that tell
Of happy days and hours, whose spell
Has not yet passed away ;
When hearts were light and spirits high,
And hope knew not that it could die,
In childhood's joyous day.
We see them gleam. Ah, yes ! they come
All freshness from our first loved home
With clear and soothing ray.
And though storms mar the summer blue,
Though some are false, and some untrue,
They speak with hope and say—
There still are friends for friendship's smile,
And joys that tedious hours beguile ;
And hearts for love, and eyes whose light
Can guide in passion's deepest night :
The hidden future yet may be
A sweet dream made reality.

Awake then, thought ! recall the past
Gone hours from their dark tomb :
Strip their pale garments from them fast,
And give them life's fresh bloom.
Let not thy erring pinions stray
Where sleeps one sad or gloomy day ;
But wing with steady course thy flight
Among the happy, joyous, bright,
Which quickly sped without a sigh,
And bring them in all freshness nigh.
But sweep not back with rapid wing
O'er years long gone—to-day
From recent scenes the fragments bring
Ere they quite pass away ;
Of Summer days and Summer hours,
Of murm'ring streams and shady bowers,
And skies all stainless blue ;
And build into a simple rhyme
These wavelets on the stream of time
In eighteen fifty-two.
Let these be thine—the wild and free,
The shell-strewn shore, the restless sea ;
The crested ocean dark and deep ;
The mountain forms, the sunlit steep ;
The quiet glen where self-sown flowers
Intwine themselves to Dryad's bowers,

And cooling shades protect the seat
Where skilful love made love's retreat.
Intwine from these a chaplet gay
For mem'ry's treacherous brow ;
Perchance upon some future day,
When time has sped a long, long way,
One reading these rude lines may say
All comes back even now.

I would not stray from this sweet shade
Of quiet glen and woodland glade :
From mountain high the spirit's home,
From winding stream and ocean's foam ;
No, not in thought ; but yet I may
Recall awhile that former day,
When one sweet voice, before unknown,
Broke forth in music all its own,
And woke sweet mem'ries which console
The lonely and too thoughtful soul.

Time sped ! I heard that voice again
Where towns were all forgot ;
It bade me welcome to Plas Hên,
A lovely quiet spot.
A sweet retreat,—a joyous home
Girt round with woods ;—the crested foam
Of ocean stretching far away

Seems with the dancing trees to play;
And down the opening glade
Foams the wild stream, and salmon leap,
And richly-scented woodbines creep
Among the quiet shade;
And banks are strewn with ferns and flowers,
And branches twine delightful bowers
Where we may lie and dream :
While hope with fairy footstep brings
Her visions of a thousand things
Down by the "Haunted Stream."
Unfettered, bounding thought is there,
While castles rise built in the air
Till all things happy seem.
I wish they would not fall and fade,
But last as beautiful as made !
I wish they would not flee away,
But stand as they were built for aye !
It may not be ! earth's visions still
Are changing as our wayward will !

Turn now, my wand'ring Muse, thy flight
Down by the wild sea shore, and 'light
On rude Pen-y-Chain's head, and tell
How looks the sea-bird's citadel
Round which they skim with startled cry,

As comes th' intruding stranger nigh.
Outstretched before it lies the deep,
Behind the mountains high ;
Rude ocean foams against the steep
Up whose rough side it may not leap ;
But falls again in tears that weep
Since it so low must lie ;
While o'er it rises cliff and hill,
And lofty summit tow'ring still
To kiss the lofty sky.
Bright shines the sun, and hours flit on,
And softly steal away ;
As airy clouds go one by one
In April's fresh'ning day ;
That leave no track nor mark when gone
To shew their free, wild way.
There beaming, happy faces meet,
And friendship sits by friendship's seat ;
And love perchance its influence lends
To make still dearer, cherish'd friends.
Now Carrie tends the lighted fire,
Till vexed with smoke and heat,
Her wearied patience seems to tire ;
She seeks some cool retreat,
And leaves her cooking half undone
To others in the broiling sun.

By yonder streaming veil I know
Who looks upon the waves below,
And hums the flying hours away
By mingling with the chanting bay
Sweet airs of some loved tune :
Bright beams her eye with colour true,
Reflecting back the ocean's hue
Caught from a sky of June.

On fly the thoughts ! away they go
To seek the bridal day ;
Joyous, yet tinged with shades of woe,
Which quickly pass away—
Like heat drops with a warning sound,
Which live but till they touch the ground.

'Tis Katie's day—a happy bride !
And beauty's smiling train
Gladly attends and stands beside
Where love asserts its reign ;
And airy forms and phantoms glide
From each excited brain.

See Carrie there, with sunny smile
And laughter-speaking face !
Save when some dark'ning clouds awhile
With angry frown we trace.

Ah ! let them go and fly away,
I know they have not long to stay,
They suit not well her grace !
For kind as any she can be,
With bounding heart all light and free,
And foremost in the race
To wake the feelings true and deep,
Which perish not, and never sleep,
Of friendship, or of love ;
But only burn with brighter fires
While the bright spirit still inspires
Which taught them first to move.

And Leonora, too, is seen
Attending on the bridal queen.
Deep-seated love expands, and fear
As draws the time of parting near.
No wonted laughter fills her eyes ;
Depression's weight upon her lies ;
Her spirit's fail ; and why ?
Her thoughts to the lone future stray,
And all is dark along the way ;
She dreads the last good-bye.
With Katie gone comes mental strife—
A home without its light and life.

But why is Hennie sad to-day ?

Hennie whose happy smile !
Can drive dull sorrow far away
And lonely hours beguile.
Why do the checked tears well-nigh start ?
Why sad and heavy feels the heart ?
Where have her spirits flown ?
The past and future wildly blend,
And rising doubts their shadows lend,
Her thoughts are not her own.
They skim the vows of friendship past
And wonder whether such will last.

But why, my Muse, delay so long
To weave into your fitful song
A tribute to the Bride ?
She ought to be the first to share
Thy praise to-day—her virtues are
Acknowledged far and wide.
See ! how she stands with modest grace,
And youth and beauty on her face,
In all her maiden pride.
Tell of her charms and goodness now
The bridal wreath surrounds her brow.
Sing of her first pure love, which woke
With a new life, and trembling broke
Its cold reserve, and wandered free,

Lost in a fresh-found sympathy.
And all that after dream whose hue
Could tinge the future life anew.
'Twere vain to try! We fain would please,
But cannot reach such heights as these.
How should the Muse unfold its wing,
Such high and lofty themes to sing?
How tell the restless lover's part;
Or secrets of a maiden's heart?
The fickle stream of love's strong tide
Did never in smooth courses glide—
Its ways are all its own.
Untaught ourselves, we cannot teach
True love—it is beyond our reach,
'Tis felt ere it is known!

St. George, I may not sing of thee
With Hennie flirting fearfully:
Nor Mouse, who gave his chance away
Upon that happy bridal day:
Nor musing Shepherd, half undone,
Dazzled by rays from beauty's sun:
Nor Fanny, with her open book;
Nor Mother, with her pensive look;
Nor Father, whose knit thoughtful brow
Speaks—"Yes! my child will leave me now!"

These only each by name I try
To mention as I pass them by ;
Because I have not time
To linger by the gliding stream
Beneath the shade, and idly dream
And weave my wayward rhyme.

The feast is spread, but who shall say
The rich repast of that glad day ?
Attempt not e'en to tell a part
Where plenty twines itself with art.
But don't omit to speak a word
Of what was kindly seen and heard
Around that festive board.
Tell how the husband speech confessed
He felt all happy, joyous, blessed,
With her his soul adored.
And how St. George rose up to say,
When from his throne the sun
Departed at the close of day
To rest from labours done :
Then in the skies, all black with night,
The moon appears, and stars so bright
Come cheering us with borrowed light
From him whose course is run.
So when the bridal sun has gone

And left the feelings sad and lone
Her moon and stars shine bright ;
Driving away the thoughts once sad ;
Making the sunken spirits glad,
The heavy heart all light.
Oh ! for a star true as that spark,
Which in night's circle deep and dark
Shines ever an unerring mark
To tell the frozen pole !
Oh ! for a star like this to guide
Our course across time's stormy tide,
And on life's ocean, trackless, wide,
To steer the doubting soul !
One that the deepest love inspires,
Where we might light our altar fires,
And constant vigils keep !
Where free devotion's stream might pour
Its wonted homage, and adore,
And joyous passion weep ;
When hopes, and fears, and dangers past,
Made faithful love more prized at last !
But, gentle Hennie, kindly tell,
Nor curious questions chide,
Whether induced by some glad spell
St. George got up and spoke so well
When standing at thy side ?

" Moon-struck," or love-inspired—did he
Not owe some happy thought to thee ?

But pause, my Muse ! nor venture near
To watch the held, yet starting tear.
Rest thy wild flight, nor wander nigh
To listen to the parting sigh.
Let every shade of sorrow's hue
Leave the clear sky all stainless blue
Where thought may freely rove ;
And build her castles, but if wise
She will ere their proud turrets rise
The first foundation prove.
This should be tested, strong and sure,
One that will long, long time endure.
What better lasts than love ?
Here faith would build her hopes : may they,
If truthful, never pass away ;
But brighten till their latest breath,
Then fade in the calm sleep of death.

Summer Seat by the Haunted Stream, July, 1852.

———

To Rose,

On her Coming-of-Age, May 9th.

METHINKS I stand on Berwyn's lofty height,
    At waking dawn, on this glad ninth of May;
When morning blushes from her eastern home,
And laughs away grim darkness from the sky;
And with her lightning fingers, as she goes,
Picks from her way the fragments of black night,
And on the trees, obscured with rising mist,
With dainty touch her rainbow colours hangs;
And with her smile makes earth look beautiful.

Along the heathered mountain's barren slopes
The morning in unwonted brightness lies.
Pure sparkling dewdrops glisten all around;
Fresh tiny streamlets prattle as they run;
"We go," say they, "down from our mountain home,
For in the vale they keep glad holiday."

From cwm and glen those prattling streamlets come;
From lonely spring and dripping mossy bed,
Till mingling into one they leap the rock,

And foam and eddy in the pool below.
Through meadows green, fresh with the breath of Sp
By early flowers in warm and sheltered nooks;
By ferns just budding into fuller life,
With ever restless motion on they go.

Llangynnog's deep ravine and village passed,
They reach Llangedwyn, where among the trees
[27]Stands in repose Sir Watkin's stately home.
Sir Watkin, chief of Wallias valiant sons,
Tracing his lineage from a hundred kings,
And on his shield the eagle bears which waved
Upon the banners of a prince renowned,
When Owain Gwynedd marched to victory!

Then on they go till Llan-y-blodwell's spire,
New and unusual rises on the view,
And pass with chanting voice the garden shade,
So tempting to the staid Divine, to sit
And ponder over subtle arguments,
Till lost in thought and mysteries unsolved.

And now they rest, not wearied in their course,
But lulled almost to slumber by the spell
Which spreads a charm around Bryn Tanat's hoı
" Dear old Bryn Tanat," whose fair queen to-day
Claims friendly greetings, loyal, loving, true!

" Warm and truthful thoughts come to thee
   On this joyous natal day ;
Thoughts which wish thee many blessings
   Never to decay.

" Peaceful be thy pathway onward,
   Opening still all bright and clear !
Let a golden future greet thee
   With each changing year !

" Rose, the queen of all the garden !
   Queen, with all its blushing grace !
Sov'reign thou in hearts around thee
   With thy winning face !

" Through the years of childhood upwards,
   Many blessings have been thine.
Lo ! they speak from the great Father,
   ' Make thy young heart Mine.'

" Now to womanhood arrivèd,
   Safe in His protecting power ;
Ne'er forget whose arm can shield thee
   In temptation's hour.

" And thus blessed, thy days all happy,
   Kept by Him till life is past ;
May His Spirit guide thee onward
   To thy rest at last."

E

In Memoriam.

TO RHO.

I SIT down on the brook side
    And see the waters run,
As they sport among the pebbles,
    And sparkle in the sun.
I watch their restless motion
    As they eddy to and fro ;
And from their gentle murmur
    There rises—Rho, Rho, Rho !

I watch them on the rapids ;
    When strong and angry grown
They run with noisy footstep,
    And smite the thwarting stone.
I listen to their voices
    As they foam with rushing flow ;
And their wild, and self-taught music
    Is chanting—Rho, Rho, Rho !

I follow in the meadows,
   .And see them wind about ;
Where hangs the brittle alder,
   And lurks the speckled trout :
Where sweetly-scented violet
   And modest primrose grow :
Their sound dies to a whisper,
   But still 'tis—Rho, Rho, Rho !

I give loose to my fancy,
   And let the spirit roam ;
Where lightning thought is leaping
   In its free and boundless home. ·
I'm lost to all around me ;
   Yet as I dreaming go,
I hear the heart's deep murmur ;
   'Tis sighing—Rho, Rho, Rho !

And when the golden sunset,
   With all its crimson fires,
Is gath'ring still intenser,
   Ere the great King expires :
I watch those airy cloud forms
   Sail through the golden glow :
But my lonely heart is yearning
   For rest, with—Rho, Rho, Rho !

In Memoriam.

TO MOTHER,

After the Birth of her first Baby-Boy, May, 1869.

THROUGH woman's sorrow deep and full
　　Our God has spared thee my own Rho;
To Him our first, and heartfelt thoughts,
　　In gratitude should go.

And may His Presence, and His love,
　　Which kept and shielded thee in pain,
Be in its fulness round thee still;
　　Till thou art strong again.

And shine about thy ev'ry path,
　　Throughout a long and peaceful life;
Till thou, in Christ art safe at last—
　　My lov'd and trusted wife!

Health to our boy! may God pour down
　　His Holy Spirit from above;
· And teach the heart, while young, to know
　　The Saviour's mighty love.

Till Spirit taught his thoughts shall soar
　　From earthly things, and count them loss;
And he in truth and heart shall be
　　A soldier of the Cross.

Health to our boy ! for thy dear sake ;
　God's gift—a mother's joy to fill,
And make thy trusting, loving heart
　More blest and happy still.

Watch'd by thy ever-anxious love ;
　And dearer still—thy strength and pride !
May he be kept with thee to share
　Life's golden eventide.

And when life's chequered race is o'er,
　And all its changing scenes are past ;
May he, and you, and I be found
　Before the throne at last.

------

[29]MOTHER'S BIRTHDAY.

Sung at her Bedroom Door, October 23rd, 1878.

A WAKE ! awake, with joyful strain !
　　Awake at early dawn !
To welcome mother home again,
　And greet her birthday morn.

Five darling pets will do their parts,
　A mother's love to win ;
Five darling pets, with longing hearts,
　Are waiting to come in.

The sickly one, though far away
   With nurse down at the sea,
Sends fondest greetings, too, to-day ;
   And kisses sweet to thee.

We wish thee many, many more
   Returns of this glad day ;
We hope for many joys in store,
   And sunshine on thy way.

May God long spare thee, mother dear !
   To us—and us to thee ;
And may we all, year after year,
   More true and loving be.

MOTHER'S BIRTHDAY.

Sung at her Bedroom Door, October 23rd, 1879.

WE are coming ! we are coming
   To wish our mother joy !
Feff, Sissie, Fee, May, Agatha,
   And little Digby boy.
Listen, mother ! dearest mother !
   To what we have to say ;
Many happy—very happy—
   Returns of this glad day !

MOTHER'S BIRTHDAY.

Sung at her Bedroom Door, October 23rd, 1880.

A ROUSE thee, sweetest mother!
  Thy children all are here;
Kept safely by God's goodness
  Throughout another year.

Since last upon thy birthday
  We woke thee up with song;
Rich blessings, upon blessings,
  Have strewn our path along.

But this we deem the richest,
  Our leaping hearts to fill
With joy to overflowing,
  That thou art with us still.

We give thee, dearest mother!
  More than our words can say,
A joyous, loving greeting
  On this thy natal day.

God guard thee! may His goodness
  In fulness round thee spread;
And all His choicest blessings
  Be shower'd upon thy head.

Still may He keep thee safely,
    Through years and years to come :
The life—the brightest sunshine—
    The joyspring of our home.

TO MOTHER.

WAKE lightly from thy slumbers
        On this thy natal day :
Give God thy heartfelt praises ;
    A year has passed away :
Another year, whose mercies prove
His gracious and abiding love.

About thy path He watched thee ;
    His tender care we trace ;
Thy deep, soft eye is brighter,
    New health is on thy face :
And as thou treadest up the hill
Of life, fresh visions open still.

And may the very brightest
    That ever met the gaze ;
Free from corroding sorrow,
    Free from obscuring haze,
Be thine ! till in a clearer day
The best of earth shall pass away.

While here, may He still lead thee
Along the path of right :
His word thy rule of action ;
His Spirit thy true light.
Yes ! onward still, till all divine
The Christian life within thee shine !

And when thy days are ending,
And all their troubles past ;
May no rude doubt disturb thee,
No gloomy shade be cast :
But safe upon thy Saviour's breast
May all be calm repose and rest.

TO MOTHER.
1883.

I RESTED on the turf-clad seat,
  Above the smiling, circling bay,
Where hoary crags morn's blushes meet ;
And saw proud ocean at my feet
  Go stretching far away.

And restless, as that restless sea,
  My thoughts went speeding to and fro ;
I pictured life all bright with thee,
From cares and clouding sorrow free :
  'Tis twenty years ago.

Though dark the future then with fear,
   I hoped one day to call thee wife ;
And find thee growing still more dear,
With every swiftly passing year,
   In trust and love for life.

That cloud of fear passed on its way ;
   God's hand has been directing all ;
From darkness He brings light—then day
Smiles where in gloom the darkness lay ;
   He rules things great and small.

He has been good to you and me ;
   And very many blessings given.
From untold ills our lives are free ;
By His unerring wisdom, we
   Are guided on towards heaven.

He has been good ! our home is blessed
   With varied comforts ; and around
. Our children flourish, loved, caressed ;
To us the sweetest and the best,
   With health and spirits crowned.

He gave, and He can keep them still,
   Where'er their lot in life is cast ;
Can guide them through this world of ill,
And give them strength and grace, until
   He lead them home at last.

He has been good ! when sorrow fell,
 Increasing almost to dismay ;
'Twas life or death—for none could tell ;
Faith whispered, "He does all things well:"
 The danger passed away.

And now a cloud appears again,
 And takes the sunshine from the scene ;
Fear conquers faith, and all the plain
Of life is dull with mist and rain ;
 No sunshine gleams between.

This cloud may pass, or deeper grow
 With living torture on the brain ;
We see not now why it is so ;
Enough ! hereafter we shall know,
 When He makes all things plain.

All is not dark ! the blackest cloud
 That stains life's azure sky above ;
Where lightning flash, and thunders loud
Are heard, is but the passing shroud
 Of God's eternal love.

Look up and trust Him ! since that love
 Will never send one needless pain ;
He trains us for the life above ;
His visitations all will prove
 Our everlasting gain.

No stroke comes from the Father's rod,
　Which is not needed in the strife,
Found in the way by martyrs trod,
And all the faithful sons of God,
　Who win the crown of life.

There is a home, where free from pain,
　When life's sore trials all are o'er,
The gathered saints with Christ shall reign;
Where loved and lost shall meet again,
　And partings be no more.

To that blest home look forward still ;
　On God's great love cast all thy care ;
He will His promises fulfil,
And bring thine own, through good and ill,
　At last to meet thee there.

Before the Reaper comes, we pray
　That God may His great goodness show;
And spare thy life, and day by day,
Clear rising doubts and fears away,
　And grace and strength bestow.

Add many joyous years to thee ;
　And happy birthdays as they come ;
Restore thy health, and set thee free
From anxious thoughts ; so thou shalt be
　The light of our glad home.

TO MOTHER.
October 23rd, 1884.

I USED to love the Spring-time
  All fresh with life and song ;
And dream upon the future
  With expectation strong.
I wandered 'mong wild flowers
  Where rippling streamlets flow,
And heard with nature's music
  The loving voice of Rho.

And through the gloomy dimness
  Of yet unfolding years,
Hope changed to rainbow colours,
  The hazy mist of fears ;
And in the dreamy stillness,
  When thoughts intenser grow,
There rose out of that silence
  The loving voice of Rho.

But now the Autumn warneth
  By far and wide decay,
That earth's best beauty changes—
  Her glories pass away :
So life's most cherish'd pleasures
  Will cloy, or fade, or go ;
But yet unchang'd remaineth
  The loving voice of Rho.

While "love and trust" unshaken
    Rule over heart and will;
Though all is changing round us
    One thing is constant still :
Through good report and evil,
    Through joy, or grief, or woe,
There comes, in sweetest accents,
    The loving voice of Rho.

TO RHO.

*   *   *   *   *

'TIS so on earth ! for never yet
    Had it a cloudless day,
Whose sun did not in darkness set,
And for black night make way.
Nay ! on its bluest, clearest skies
Unthought-of storms will often rise.
'Tis so with life ! around our home
Griefs, fears, and disappointments roam.
They enter there, if God so will,
And speak, when hushed the soul is still.
They are but mercies kindly given
To teach there is no rest but Heaven.

In that glad home, nor death, nor sin
To break its peace will enter in;
But sin's destructive power will cease,
And then will come eternal peace.

Not Death, but Sleep.

Written after the Funeral of Minna Evadne Edwards, who died May 6th, 1873, aged 3 years.

"SHE is not dead, but sleepeth," He
    Once said Whose word is life—Whose breath
Brings hope and blessed peace, but she,
    The maid, lay still in death.

He stood within the silent room,
    Where all was ghastly stiff repose,
His word and touch dispell'd the gloom,
    The sleeping maid arose.

I hear that voice again to-day,
    As to the open grave we tread,
In soothing tones it comes to say,
    "The sleeper is not dead."

Is this not true? look up and see,
    The springing, teeming earth is rife,
With bursting shell, with budding tree,
    All signs of waking life.

Not Death, but Sleep.

The morning sheen is all around,
  The morning light is on the hill,
And nature's voice in one glad sound,
  Proclaims her living still.

The reaper came, he took the flower,
  Now dearest to the mother's heart ;
In bitterness she felt the power,
  Of the destroyer's dart.

Faith falls before that stunning blow,
  It cannot rise to see the light ;
Too full of grief the heart lies low,
  For all is dark as night.

The thoughts are on the open tomb,
  Not on that better, brighter scene,
Where flowers put on immortal bloom,—
  Death's shadow lies between.

" The resurrection and the life
  I am," He said, Who came to save,
And conquer'd in the mighty strife,
  And burst the fetter'd grave.

Through Him the lost are ours again,
  For faith looks for the world to come,
Where we with them still hope to reign,
  In that bright sinless home.

There, even now, thy lost one soars,
  Before the throne on angel wings,
And in the light of love adores,
  And with the seraph sings.

Weep not ! it was thy Father's will,—
  We lay thy lov'd one down to rest,
In gentle slumber, safe and still,
  On her Redeemer's breast.

There to be kept with tend'rer care,
  Than even thy fond mother's love,—
There kept till thou art called to share
  With her full joys above.

Crux Mihi Anchora.

(Suggested by above words on a Bands' Case presented to me.)

SAFE by the Cross no doubts arise,
  No fears disturb the breast ;
Our home is made beyond the skies,
  There is the longed-for rest.

F

For this fair Christian soldier fight,
   Since death will cast its shade ;
Thy flashing eye will lose its light,
   And beauty's tints will fade.

Safe by the Cross securely dwell,
   And let the world sweep by ;
Its tide may heave, and burst, and swell,
   Thou canst its strength defy.

If lifting up thy thoughts above,
   Thou learnest day by day
There is a world of endless love ;
   While this will pass away.

Safe by the Cross ! with Christ alone,
   And hope and strength divine ;
All powerful at Jehovah's throne,
   Each blessing shall be thine.

There be thy rest ! and may His power,
   Who breaks the spell of death,
Grant Thee that gracious, mightiest dower—
   His re-creating breath.

The Way of Life.

STEEP is the way that leads to God,
  By few that way is bravely trod ;
Be this thy fear, lest it should be
The better way unknown to thee.

Steep is that way ! ah, then beware !
Lest other ways be all thy care,
Here lies the path from sloth and sin,
This thou must tread the crown to win.

Steep is the way ! awake ! arise !
And seek true rest beyond the skies.
By grace—by faith this way may be
A daily path cf life to thee.

Steep is the way ! but not too steep
For those whom Jesus calls from sleep.
If grace and faith within thee reign
To live is Christ—to die is gain.

New Year.

FOR Thy mercies broadly cast,
    Thro' the year so lately past ;
For Thy blessings, day by day,
Freely scatter'd round our way ;
Safely kept thro' good and ill,
For Thy love was with us still ;
We would raise our song to Thee,
Ever blessed Trinity.

Thro' the year now just begun,
Keep us till its sands have run ;
With Thy wings above us spread,
By Thy Presence onward led ;
Strengthened by Thy pow'r within,
To resist and vanquish sin ;
Our glad song shall rise to Thee,
Ever blessed Trinity.

In Thy courts we meet to-day,
For Thy special grace to pray;
Take us to Thy guardian care,
Let us all Thy blessing share;
With Thy heav'nly grace endue,
Every heart create anew;
Draw us by Thy pow'r to Thee
Ever blessed Trinity.

Gracious Father, by Thy might
Keep us in the path of right;
Blessed Saviour, by Thy love
Lead us to Thy home above;
Holy Spirit, from on high
Guide, and guard, and sanctify;
Bring us all to rest in Thee,
Ever blessed Trinity.

Advent.

THERE sounds a note of warning,
  It is the herald's cry,—
The Lord of life is coming,
  His advent day is nigh!
He comes! the Judge upon His throne!
He comes! His waiting Church to own!

Be ready then and waiting,
　　Thy absent Lord to see !
The day of thy redemption
　　That advent day shall be !
He comes ! the Judge upon His throne !
He comes ! His waiting Church to own !

Now with the world's false pleasure
　　Renounced and put away,
Thy heart shall leap with gladness,
　　As dawns the advent day ;
He comes ! the Judge upon His throne !
He comes ! His waiting Church to own !

Arise with expectation,
　　Behold, times' gloomy sky
Grows bright with hope and promise !
　　The advent day is nigh ;
He comes ! the Judge upon His throne !
He comes ! His waiting Church to own !

WATCH and wait ; the stream is rolling
　　Swiftly towards the end of time,
Bearing all with rapid motion
　　Onward to that day sublime,
When will come the midnight cry,
Wake ! the Bridegroom Judge is nigh !

Watch and wait ! for as the lightning
  Flashing o'er the wide wide sea,
At a moment unexpected,
  Shall the Saviour's coming be ;
Then will rise the midnight cry,
Wake ! the Bridegroom Judge is nigh !

Watch and wait in expectation !
  Ready for that dreadful day,
When the sure abiding heaven,
  As a scroll shall pass away,
And be heard the midnight cry,
Wake ! the Bridegroom Judge is nigh !

Watch and wait ! but safe in Jesus,
  He alone can keep us when
His appearing shall with terror
  Seize the failing hearts of men,
As goes forth the midnight cry,
Wake ! the Bridegroom Judge is nigh !

Watch and wait with lamps all ready !
  Sanctified in heart and life,
Looking for His re-appearing,
  And the end of sinful strife ;
Then 'twill be the welcome cry,
Wake ! the Bridegroom Judge is nigh !

Christmas.

(Written for " Lyra Messianica.")

NIGHT spreads her sable veil
   Across the stainless sky ;
And one by one each twinkling star
Peeps from its silent home afar,
   Tempting the wandering eye
To rest—while thought in vision soars,
And lost in wonderment adores.

But lo ! the vaulted dome
   Is filled with light divine ;
God's Angel comes to earth to-day
With gracious news, about his way
   Celestial glories shine :
He comes to tell to fallen earth
The long-expected Saviour's birth.

Christmas.

The shepherds see the light,
   And they are sore afraid ;
They hear His voice—" Let terror cease ;
To you is born the Prince of Peace,
   And in a manger laid :
Go ! seek the Saviour—Christ the Lord,
The ever-blessed, all-adored ! "

Then wakes a mighty song
   From Angel hosts above ;
And multitudes unite to sing
The praise of their eternal King,
   And His redeeming love :
Divine and full, that wondrous sound
Goes echoing the wide world around.

" Glory to God on high,
   And on the earth be peace,
Good will to men"—so swells the strain,
Hope visits this lost world again—
   Hope that will never cease ;
While Jesu's grace, and Jesu's love,
Call fallen man to rest above.

The Epiphany.

WHAT a star was that whose splendour
    Seen above Euphrates' tide,
Safely led the wond'ring Magi
    To the Infant Saviour's side !

O'er the barren rocks of Edom,
    O'er the desert's burning sand,
Onward to fair Zion's city,
    Onward from their Eastern land.

But a brighter light has risen,
    Jacob's star, with healing ray,
Risen on the Gentile nations,
    Herald of a perfect day.

Still it shines with growing lustre
    Unto earth's remotest bound,
Spreading life, and free salvation,
    Where sin's gloomy reign is found.

Light divine ! draw our affections,
   Teach us the right way to see,
Lead us from our nature's darkness
   To the better life in Thee.

(Written for " Lyra Mystica," and favourably noticed by the " Saturday Review." Re-published in " The Church Seasons.")

BEYOND the barren mountain range,
   Where Hor lifts up his sacred head,
And buried lies in myst'ry strange,
As years work out their silent change,
   The city of the dead.

Where proud Euphrates day by day
   Winds through the plain, or sleeping lies ;
The watching Magi nightly pray,
And seek the future's hidden way
   From planet-lighted skies.

Through clear unclouded midnight air,
   On vast infinity's dark page ;
With deepest skill, and constant care,
They read the golden letters there
   That wax not old with age.

The Epiphany.

Lo ! as they gaze with deep intent,
   A star more brilliant than the rest,
The herald of some great event,
Moves through the gilded firmament,
   Onward towards the West.

Then came the sound tradition brought
   From Peor's top in days of old ;
What time the Seer, entrancèd, caught
Prophetic power, and Spirit taught,
   The future did unfold.

" A sceptre shall from Israel rise ;
   A star from Judah doubly blest ! "
And now before their wond'ring eyes
This brilliant meteor walks the skies,
   Still on towards the West.

Where'er it leads, that fiery light
   Unhidden by the blaze of day,
And marking with intenser might
The darkness of the deeper night,
   They follow on the way.

With morning's blush ; when sunsets fade ;
   On over rock, and steep, and wild,
By palm and cedar tree and shade,
Till in the homely manger laid,
   They find the Royal Child.

Intruding doubts away they fling ;
  Unheeding the unwonted stir,
They from their costly treasures bring
Free offerings to the Infant King—
  Gold, Frankincense and Myrrh.

Gold shadows forth His royalty ;
  While Frankincense His priesthood shows ;
And Myrrh that He shall buried be ;
And so the wondrous mystery
  With deeper meaning grows.

Oh ! for some holy light enshrined
  In God's dark ways, or Holy Word,
To break upon each darkened mind
With Spirit power, till all may find
  That Saviour, Christ the Lord.

Till walking in a living way
  To holier purpose we arise ;
And on His Altar day by day
Our thoughts and best affections lay,
  A willing sacrifice.

The Crucifixion.

(Written for " Lyra Messianica.")

HEAVEN and earth are hushed in silence,
　　Watching for the latest throe ;
Christ, the God-man Saviour, suffers
　　On the Cross intensest woe :
　　　　Jesus dies upon the tree
　　　　In extremest agony !

Baffled in the desert's struggle,
　　And Gethsemane's dark hour ;
Now Satanic hosts assemble,
　　Sin assails with all its power :
　　　　Jesus dies upon the tree
　　　　In extremest agony !

In the garden, in the desert,
　　In His life work not alone ;
But the light, till now unclouded,
　　Fades around His Father's throne :
　　　　Jesus dies upon the tree
　　　　In extremest agony !

Darker than the sudden darkness,
   On the troubled soul within,
Deeper, denser, more oppressive,
   Rises up that cloud of sin :
      Jesus dies upon the tree
      In extremest agony!

From eternity approving,
   Love shone from the Father's brow ;
Never absent from His Presence,
   But the Father leaves Him now!
      Jesus dies upon the tree
      In extremest agony!

Deadlier than the body's torture,
   Than the sinking, fainting frame,
Hopeless, crushing, overwhelming,
   Growing desolation came :
      Jesus dies upon the tree
      In extremest agony!

Who shall tell the depth of feeling
   Echoed through the worlds on high,
Full, intense, unmeasured anguish
   Spoken in that bitter cry,
      Rising wildly from the tree—
      " Why hast Thou forsaken Me?"

Gaze with wond'ring adoration
　At the Cross the Saviour bore !
Gaze until the heart is melted !
　Lo ! it speaks—"Go, sin no more ! "
Look, my soul, look up and see !
　　　Jesus dies upon the tree
　　　In extremest agony ;
　　　Jesus dies, dies thus for thee !

Easter Day.

(Written for " Lays of the Sanctuary.")

COME to the grave to mourn and weep
　Where Jesus calmly lies ;
Where list'ning silence, still and deep,
　Bids holiest thought arise.
Tread softly, for among the dead
With careless step 'twere wrong to tread ;
Or vex with aught that home so dread,
　Where mirth and laughter dies.

But see ! the morning dawns, and day
   Steals on the track of night ;
The shapeless masses move away
   As spreads the tinting light ;
And day awakes—another week
Breaks with its cares, and sad we seek
The dead ; but lo ! the living speak,
   Clad in pure robes of white.

" Why seek the living 'mong the dead ?
   The Saviour did not die
To make this dismal tomb His bed,
   Where He for aye must lie.
Heard ye no shout ? The far worlds ring,
Angels attend the risen King,
His triumph over death shall bring
   His own Redeemed nigh."

To-day is spread a Holy Feast,
   With willing hearts obey ;
Draw near with faith, nor let the least
   In hope, turn cold away.
By the known symbols of His love
The mind is drawn to things above,
And strength and grace imparted prove
   We meet the Lord to-day !

   G

This is our day ! We will rejoice,
   Sin reigns in us no more :
Grace triumphs—let us lift our voice
   The Saviour to adore.
He broke the cruel tyrant's sway ;
He took the sting of death away ;
Let us with gratitude obey
   Till this short life is o'er.

And when through death's dark gate we go
   To happier worlds unknown,
Where we mysterious love shall know,
   And ruling wisdom own :
Divinely taught His praise to sing,
Spontaneous then our thoughts will spring
To Him, our God, Redeemer, King,
   On His eternal throne.

Ascension.

HARK ! for the shout of triumph
   Through all Creation rings ;
Angelic hosts are greeting
   The risen King of kings.
O'er Death and Hell victorious,
   All power to Him is given ;
The Conq'ror of all Conq'rors,
   Ascendeth up to Heaven.

Ascension.

Lift up ye gates eternal !
  And be ye lifted high
Ye doors from everlasting
  The guardians of the sky !
Admit the King of glory,
  The King Who comes to reign !
Who is this King of Glory ?
  The Lamb for sinners slain.

The Lamb Who meekly suffered,
  And in the sinner's stead
Died on the Cross as guilty,
  Now risen from the dead ;
Rais'd by the power immortal,
  Rais'd never more to die :
Lift up ye gates eternal,
  Ye doors be lifted high !

Admit the King of glory,
  The Lord of Hosts is He ;
The Lord supreme for ever
  To all eternity.
Let Heaven's united chorus
  Its glad hosannas sing
To Christ, the Lord of glory—
  Christ, the redeeming King !

The Gate of Life.

(Written for " Lays of the Sanctuary.")

WHY should we fear to die?
   Has death so sharp a sting
That every sign which shows Him near
Must force a sigh, or start a tear,
   And gloomy visions bring?
Is there no ray—from endless day,
To quell the Spectre Form, and light the dismal way?

'Tis painful, true! to leave
   All that we love so well:
Home—where our young affections grew;
Where love is strong, and hearts are true,
   And hallow'd mem'ries dwell:
As silently—We droop and die,
And feel that none can save; no aiding hand is nigh.

The best, 'tis said, go first :
　So have I seen the day
Which brightest shone the soonest fade ;
Ere noon-tide came, dark clouds and shade
　Took the glad light away.
From harm and care—The young and fair
Depart—the loved are gone ; our dream alone is there !

Gone through the " Gate of Life,"
　To where the ransomed live,
Free from the tainting breath of sin ;
Where perfect rest and peace begin ;
　Such as our God can give :
Cleans'd from each stain—Then death is gain,
Emancipated souls in glory hence to reign.

The tyrant's spectral Form
　Becomes the " Gate of Life ; "
Since on the Cross the Saviour shed
His costly blood, and for the dead
　Engaged in mortal strife
With Death and Hell—Their power to quell,
Till He the Victor rose, and they the vanquish'd fell.

Oh ! where then is thy sting,
   Dread King of Terrors, where ?
Let faith arise and wing its way,
And realize eternal day,
   And see the ransom'd there,
Who from thy might—And clouded night
Have risen into joy, and endless realms of light.

By thee the pathway leads
   Up to our home above ;
Thy touch is but a signal given,
When threads which bind to earth are riven
   By God's unchanging love :
His hand, not thine—His power divine
Calls up a soul from earth in blissful courts to shine.

He only wounds to heal ;
   He smites that He may save ;
He gives to feeble faith a wing,
And takes from thee thy dreaded sting,
   And terrors from the grave :
Each chosen son—His warfare done,
Hears the triumphant shout—another crown is won !

God's Word Written.

WITHIN Thy Holy Word
     What endless love I see,
For Mercy, gracious Lord,
     And Justice meet in Thee ;
          Thou dost declare—I need not fear,
          If Thou art near—My sin to bear.

Oh ! give me light to read
     The promises divine ;
They meet my ev'ry need,
     By faith they all are mine,
          For Thou hast said—Each hungry one,
          May feed upon—The living bread.

Then let me mark and learn,
     And inwardly digest,
Till all my longings turn
     To Thy most perfect rest,
          When sin shall cease—His darts to throw,
          And all shall know—Eternal peace.

So let me day by day,
     Nearer and nearer come,
As faith sees far away
     My everlasting home,
          Where seraphs raise—With love untold,
          On harps of gold—Unceasing praise.

The Sabbath.

JEHOVAH'S Sabbath this—
　　The day most truly blest ;
A type of everlasting bliss,
　　And never broken rest.

A time for prayer and praise,
　　By God in mercy given,
Snatch'd from the world engrossing days,
　　To calm our souls for heaven.

Within His temple meet,
　　And lift the heart above ;
Approach His open mercy seat,
　　And praise Him for His Love.

Check ev'ry sinful thought,
　　Let earthly cares give way ;
Gaze on the prize that Christ has bought,
　　Reserv'd in endless day.

And for that prize press on,
　　Its glory thou shalt see,
When persevering faith hath won,
　　The final victory.

Everlasting Love.

O LOVE from everlasting,
  To everlasting known !
Unbounded, free, unceasing,
  In man's redemption shown !
For Jesus suffered on the tree,
And died to set the sinner free.

I see the sight and tremble ;
  I know the sin was mine,
Which made my loving Saviour
  Endure this wrath divine ;
For Jesus suffered on the tree,
And died a sacrifice for me.

I feel my cold heart melted ;
  I gaze upon His side
And sinless body broken—
  It was for me He died !
For Jesus suffered on the tree,
And died a sacrifice for me.

No more my own, for Jesus
    Has bought me with a price !
His precious blood my ransom,
    His life the sacrifice !
For He has died upon the tree,
And shed that precious blood for me.

From earthly things forbidden,
    My selfish heart must rise ;
My life in His work hidden
    Must press towards the prize—
For Jesus died upon the tree,
And shed His precious blood for me.

Hymn

For the Institution of New Vicar, May 29th, 1879.

WE come, O Lord, to Thee,
    For special grace to-day ;
Most holy blessed Trinity
    We for Thy servant pray !

Clothe him with righteousness ;
    Thy spirit power accord ;
Grant him great boldness to confess
    His Master, Christ the Lord.

Impart the grace to teach,
  Read, visit, watch, and pray ;
Jesus, the crucified to preach,
  The life—the truth—the way.

The message of Thy love
  Poor wandering souls can win—
Salvation from the King above,
  To this world dark with sin.

So may he tend and lead
  The flock, lest any stray ;
And with unceasing labour feed
  His people day by day.

Thy will, not his, be done,
  So let him bear the cross ;
And for the sake of Thy dear Son,
  Count all things else but loss.

Thy home, Lord, with us make ;
  For good our hearts prepare,
And minister and people take
  Beneath Thy loving care.

————

Hymn

Sung at the opening of St. Chad's New Schools, 1860.

ALMIGHTY Father send
   Thy heav'nly blessing down,
Thy full approving presence lend
   Our finish'd work to crown.

Incarnate Saviour take
   Possession of this place ;
Here teach Thy little flock, and make
   Them children of Thy grace.

Eternal Spirit come,
   Thy quick'ning pow'r impart,
Create a temple for Thy home
   In every youthful heart.

Descend and here remain,
   Our light, our guide, our stay,
O'er all assert Thy gracious reign,
   And teach us day by day.

So shall the Father's might,
   The Saviour's boundless love,
The Spirit's watchful care and light,
   Lead on to realms above.

Morning.

THROUGH night's deep and solemn stillness
   Safely kept, my soul, arise !
Lift thy voice with early praises
   Now that morning lights the skies.

Lift thy voice in adoration
   To thy God—great King of kings !
Who returning health and freshness
   Daily to His children brings.

Raise, O Lord, my thoughts and feelings
   Upwards with my words to Thee ;
From the world's engrossing pleasures
   Set my tempted spirit free.

That beyond this vale of shadows
   Looking from the passing day,
I may see the King in beauty,
   And the land now far away.

And so led by brighter visions
   To new hopes and life arise,
Earnest, self-denying, pressing,
   Ever onward to the prize.

Morning.

WHEN we awake be with us, Lord,
 To lift our early thoughts to Thee ;
Breathe lessons from Thy Holy Word,
 And from temptations set us free.

Be with us through our daily strife,
 And turmoil of this world of sin ;
Keep fresh and pure the secret life
 Which gives us mastery within.

Be with us when the freezing shade
 Of passing years comes creeping on—
When mem'ries old impressions fade,
 And all the powers of life are gone.

Be with us in death's trying hour ;
 Bid rising doubts and murmurs cease ;
Surround us with Thy saving pow'r,
 And teach us how to die in peace.

Evening.

THE glories of the setting sun
   Have melted in the West;
The labours of the day are done,
   And nature sinks to rest.

Through all the day, Thy care around
   My pathway, Lord, hath been!
Thy mercies everywhere abound,
   Thy love in all is seen.

I come to thank Thee for that love,
   My grateful voice to raise,
And offer for the courts above
   My evening hymn of praise.

Before I lay me down to sleep
   I bend before Thy throne,
And with contrition full and deep,
   My sins and failings own.

Oh ! pardon every mis-spent hour,
 And all my deeds of wrong,
And keep me by Thy mighty power
 Through watches dark and long.

Let me beneath Thy sheltering care
 In peaceful slumber lie ;
Thy ever sure protection share,
 And waking find Thee nigh.

Praise.

WE come with adoration,
 O Lord of earth and heaven,
To thank Thee for Thy goodness
 And mercies largely given ;
Thy hand in all around we see
And lift our heartfelt praise to Thee.

Our daily food and raiment
 Are Thine—our health and breath ;
Thou shieldest us in danger,
 Thou guardest us from death :
We raise our thoughts, O Lord, above,
And praise Thee for Thy boundless love.

Day after day Thou bearest
With all our wayward sin ;
And day by day Thy Spirit
Is waging war within,
To set us from the tyrant free,
And give us final victory.

Our strength is only weakness—
Without Thy aiding grace,
We strive in vain to conquer,
Or run the heav'nly race ;
Unaided we must fall and fail,
In Thee we triumph and prevail.

To Thee, Almighty Father,
And Thine Incarnate Son ;
To Thee Eternal Spirit,
Most glorious Three in One ;
All thanks, and praise, and glory be,
Ador'd mysterious Trinity.

H

RHUDDLAN CASTLE.

RHUDDLAN CASTLE was built by Llewelyn ap Seisyllt, after he had invaded North Wales and slain Ædan, the King, and his four sons. He took possession of the kingdom, and made this new castle his chief residence, but was assassinated in 1021. For a time Iago usurped the government, thrusting out Grufydd, Llewelyn's son. In 1037, however, Grufydd slew Iago, and regained his father's throne, and proved himself a wise and successful ruler; but he had to flee before Harold, the Earl, acting for Edward the Confessor, who invaded North Wales, defeated the Welsh in several battles, and took and burned Rhuddlan Castle. It was afterwards restored and held by the Welsh, but in 1098 it surrendered, and came into the hands of William the Conqueror. David, son of Owain Gwynedd, attacked it in 1165, but he had to retire before the advance of Henry II. It was, however, besieged and taken, 1167, by Owain Gwynedd and his allies. It afterwards surrendered to the English, who held it until 1214, when it was retaken by Llewelyn the Great. It was again wrested from the Welsh by Edward I., who held a Parliament there. It was finally taken and dismantled by the Parliamentary forces under General Mytton, 1646.

NOTES.

1. Taliesin was one of the most famous and ancient of the Welsh Bards.

2. Iago, the rightful heir to the sovereignty of North Wales, having been set on one side on account of his youth, two rival chiefs, Cynan and Ædan, contended for the throne. Ædan proved successful. He slew Cynan in battle, A.D. 1003.

3. Ædan did not enjoy his success very long. Llewelyn ap Seisyllt, King of South Wales, invaded North Wales, slew Ædan and his four sons in battle, and took possession of the kingdom. This Llewelyn ap Seisyllt built Rhuddlan Castle, and made it his royal residence. It is recorded that "in his time the land brought forth double, that the people prospered in all their affairs, and multiplied wonderfully, that the cattle increased in great numbers, and that there was not a poor man in Wales."

4. There was a tradition among the Welsh people that their kings were descended from Brutus, son of Æneas, the Trojan.

5. Meyrick, a powerful chieftain, raised a rebellion, but Llewelyn defeated his forces in battle, and slew Meyrick with his own hand.

6. The people of South Wales rebelled against Llewelyn after he had taken up his residence in North Wales, and set up Rhun, a Scotsman of low birth, as their King. Llewelyn marched into South Wales, and in a bloody battle defeated Rhun, who afterwards was taken and slain. It was the custom of the Bards, at the great feasts, to recount in song the exploits of their Kings and Nobles.

7. Llewelyn was assassinated by Howel and Meredydd, who set up Iago as King in place of Grufydd, son of Llewelyn ; but when Grufydd arrived at manhood, he raised an army, and having defeated and slain Iago in battle, he recovered his father's throne. He soon after met the united forces of the English and Danes at Crosford, on the banks of the Severn, and entirely defeated their forces.

8. Howel, after the murder of Llewelyn, obtained the sovereignty of South Wales, but was driven out by an invasion of Grufydd. Howel, however, by means of Edwyn, brother of Leofric, Earl of Chester, raised an army and marched against Grufydd. The latter was again victorious. Edwyn was slain, and Howel saved himself by flight.

9. Edward, the Confessor, angry with Grufydd on account of the destruction of Hereford Cathedral, and the murder of the Bishop in a second incursion, ordered Harold, the Earl, to invade North Wales. Harold nearly surprised Grufydd in his Castle at Rhuddlan, but the latter just escaped with a few of his followers by ship. Disappointed at not taking Grufydd, Harold burned his castle.

10. After the death of Grufydd, Meredydd, son of Owen ap Edwyn, obtained the sovereignty of North Wales. The Castle of Rhuddlan was re-built, and by the command of William the Norman, was strengthened and fortified.

11. David, son of Owen Gwynedd, laid waste the Vale of Clwyd, A.D. 1165. He attacked Rhuddlan Castle, but had to retire before the advance of King Henry. King Henry afterwards encamped on the Berwyn, but had to retreat in consequence of a want of supplies.

12. After the retreat of the King from the Berwyn, the forces of North Wales under Owen Gwynedd ; those of South Wales under

Rhys ap Grufydd ; and those of Powys under Owen Cyfeilioc, and the sons of Madoc ap Meredydd, attacked Rhuddlan Castle, and after two months' siege, took it and levelled it to the ground.

13. Baldwin, Archbishop of Canterbury, when preaching a Crusade in Wales, stayed a while at Rhuddlan Castle.

14. After the destruction of the Castle by Owen Gwynedd, it came again into possession of the English, and was re-built and fortified. Its defence for a time was in the hands of the Earl of Chester.

15. It was taken again by Llewelyn and his brother David, A.D. 1282, and they are said to have slain all the workmen they found in it.

16. Edward I. made great preparations for invading Wales, and issued summonses that all his military tenants should meet him at Rhuddlan in the month of June. The Prelates of England, and 24 Abbots holding of the Crown, were included in these orders to send thither their services.

17. Llewelyn was slain by Adam de Francton while trying to re-join his army, which he had left for a conference in a small grove near Buillt. It is supposed he had been betrayed, and the grove surrounded by the enemy.

18. Penmaen Mawr was considered the strongest fortification the Welsh possessed, and was capable of containing 20,000 men. Dolwyddelan, a stronghold, which could only be approached on one side, held out for about two years after the others, and the Knight who brought the news of its fall to Rhuddlan, received a fee for his trouble.

19. David, after he was taken prisoner, was closely confined in Rhuddlan Castle. He made repeated requests to be allowed to see the King, but the King would not consent to an interview.

20. Edward commanded that all the Bards in Wales should be hanged by martial law, under pretence that they had incited the people to sedition. Their chief seat was in Anglesea.

21. Referring to the King's promise of a Prince, "born in their own country, who could not speak a word of English, and whose life was free from every stain."

22. Richard the Second, on his return from Ireland, stayed a short time at Rhuddlan Castle with the Earl of Northumberland, before he was betrayed to his rival Bolingbroke.

The Authorities for the Notes on Rhuddlan Castle are the following :—Welsh Chronicle, Warrington's Hist. Wales, Brut. Twysogion, Geoffrey of Monmouth, Roger de Hoveden, Matthew of Westminster, Annales Cambriæ, Rymer, Camden's Brit., Statute of Rhuddlan, &c.

23. Rose, the youngest daughter of Mrs. Perry, of Bryn Tanat ; her father died when she was quite young. When she was about 12 years old, she had a very severe attack of scarlet fever, and was unconscious for some days. I visited her during the illness, and was the first person she knew when she came to herself. We afterwards became great friends, and I generally wrote her some verses for her birthday.

24. I was returning to Killarney, one day, from the Gap of Dunloe, when a friend kindly offered me a seat in his boat to cross the lakes. The lines were suggested by a song his daughters sang while crossing.

25. The Royal Oak, now the large Hotel, at Bettws-y-Coed, was formerly only a way-side inn, with one parlour, about 14ft. square, and four or five bedrooms. On one of the doors an artist had drawn a woman, life-size, standing against the door with her arm through the staple, to prevent the door opening ; representing Lady Katherine Douglas barring the door with her arm, at Perth,

against the murderers of James I. In 1851 I was at Bettws for six weeks, with my father (the Doctor), John Fogg, an ardent fisherman; Bach, an artist; Radford, an artist, and his pupil, Tulloch; Hallewell, a captain in the army, also a sketcher, whom I afterwards saw favourably mentioned by the *Times* correspondent during the Crimean War; Hulme and Chattock, both artists. There was also " Old" Hoyle, as he was called in a friendly way. He was formerly connected with a mercantile house, but having grown too stout to attend to business comfortably, his uncle allowed him an annuity. He settled at Bettws, and became quite a part of the place, and was known to everybody. He painted a little, freely criticized the work of others, and took not unkindly to brandy and water. On Sunday, when dressed in his best attire, with a flower in his buttonhole, he was quite a picture. David Cox, too, was there, but he always had rooms at the farm. In 1851 very few tourists visited Bettws, but when I went there again for a few weeks in 1866 I found a great change. The Oak had been very much enlarged, and there were many visitors. It was on this occasion the ascent of Snowdon was made; the ladies of the party being Miss Eastlake, her cousin, and a young lady friend.

26. Plas Hên. An old mansion beautifully situated at the head of a glen opening down to the sea, through which runs the river Dwyfach. In 1852 it was occupied by the Rev. St. George Armstrong Williams, his wife, a son, St. George, and four daughters, Kate, Carrie, Leonora, and Fanny. I was there at the wedding of his eldest daughter, Kate. There were also " Mouse," an undergraduate; Hennie, a young lady from London, and other visitors. Pen-y-Chain is a lonely barren rock, much frequented by wild fowl, running out into the sea, not far from Criccieth. On this we had a picnic a few days before the wedding.

27. Llangedwyn. One of the old seats of the Wynnstay family. Now the residence of the Dowager Lady Williams Wynn.

29. Mother had been away on a visit in 1878, and only returned home for her birthday. Rho was a familiar name by which Mother was known both before and also after marriage.

30. Minna Evadne Edwards was the little daughter of the Rev. E. Edwards, Vicar of Ruabon. She died when only a little more than three years old. The morning of her funeral was a bright May morning, and as we passed along in solemn procession by the side of Wynnstay Park, under the lofty trees just budding forth in their Spring freshness, the sun shining through them, spreading light and warmth and new life all around, nature seemed to have no sympathy with death. The thoughts turned to the resurrection, and I wrote the lines for Mrs. Edwards. She, too, has since been called to her rest, mourned by the whole Parish. One of the kindest and most gentle of women, she drew to herself the good-will and affection of all who had the privilege of knowing her.

F. W. K.

Bayston Hill Vicarage,
May 19th, 1890.

www.ingramcontent.com/pod-product-compliance
Lightning Source LLC
Chambersburg PA
CBHW020756020726
47495CB00008B/2451